THE LIFE
and TIMES of a
PIONEER FAMILY

THE LIFE
and TIMES of a
PIONEER FAMILY

Written by

Cheryl Hammack

Edited By

Cheryl Hammack

Library of Congress Control Number: 2021909756

HARDBACK: 978-1-955347-58-7
PAPERBACK: 978-1-955347-57-0
EBOOK: 978-1-955347-59-4

Ordering Information:

For orders and inquiries, please contact:
1-888-404-1388
www.goldtouchpress.com
book.orders@goldtouchpress.com

Printed in the United States of America

DEDICATION
AND MEMORIAL PAGE

I want to dedicate this novel / book to my very good friend Shari Showalter. I want to always remember Shari as a very high spirited person she always had a smile on her face and she had lots of pride and very brave. Shari was a type of person you could talk to because she always listened and would always help you in any way she could even if it was just a smile on her face. For everyone who knew Shari knows she was a very special person and I will always remember Shari in just that way.

I want everyone who reads this book to know Shari lives in my book.

Shari Showalter
January 30, 1965—
October 24,2007

(WE LOVE YOU SHARI AND WILL BE MISSED BY ALL)

SECTION # 1

(PART ONE)

CHAPTER # 1

This is a story about a young pioneer family starting out for the very first time on their own. It was springtime and the year was March 27,1809. The town they lived in was Kansas city Missouri. This story begins with this young man named Rusty. Rusty was a very hard working young man always devoting his daylight hours and a few of his evening hours in the Blacksmith shop where he worked. He worked in the shop with his best friends Roger and Jeff. One day his friends thought Rusty spent to much time at the shop and needed more out of his life then just working. So his friends introduced Rusty to this young girl named Shari. Rusty was so pleased with this young lady he could only think of her as the best thing that's ever happened to him. Rusty and Shari dated each other for over two years until the love between them was so abundant they realized that they were meant for each other. It was in the fall time and the year was November 20, 1811 Rusty proposed his engagement to his lovely young lady friend. Finally spring time came and the year was May 28, 1812 Rusty married his young bride. Things were tough at first for this young newlywed couple but as they adjusted to their new lives together everything started to go well with them. Rusty was always putting some of his money away that he saved over a period of several years. Soon Rusty knew he would have to take the money he saved and purchased a small cabin with a few acres of land for his new bride and himself to live. He spent all the rest of his savings to purchase a team of oxen and a wagon for transportation as well as plowing equipment from his good friend Jeff so he could farm his own land. It was summertime and the year was June 21 1812 he quit working at the Blacksmith shop to devote more of his time to his new bride. He took a few acres of his farmland and planted them up with two high demanding cash crops. One and a half acres he planted with corn and the other acre and a half he planted with wheat. He was so proud of his crops he would spend many hours of the day tending to his fields until the day of harvest which usually didn't happened until late September or early October. He depended on his crops to make back his savings that he spent to live on. One late summer day in the month of August it was predicted that a furious storm with strong winds, large hail and possibly tornados would hit the Kansas city area. Rusty knew if he didn't do anything about his crops before the big storm all would be lost. Rusty contacted his two best friends Roger and Jeff to bring their wagons, plowing equipment, and their teams of oxen with them. Roger and Jeff knew how important the crops were to their friend but by the time Roger and Jeff gathered all their things and made it over to Rusty's farm the big storm hit. Rusty, Roger, and Jeff knew they would have to hurry if they were going to save the crops. They each took an acre of land so they could try and save as much of the crops as they could. While as the wind, hail and torrential rain came down upon them they kept on working. A few minutes later the winds quit blowing and the hail quit hitting them and when they looked up they saw this big F-3 tornado heading right towards them. They hurried to set the oxen free from the plows and they ran as fast as they could to save their own lives. Soon they made it to the barn where they stayed until the storm passed by which took only about 15 minutes from start to finish. After awhile they came out of the barn to evaluate the damage and all of Rusty's crops were destroyed even the wagons were turned upside down and all of Rusty's dreams for his crop yield were shattered. But Rusty was still blessed he still had his cabin and barn and best of all he still had his beloved bride Shari. Jobs were generally hard to find and if you were lucky enough to have had a job and leave that job for any reason it could be very hard to get their jobs back. The economy was at its lowest point.

The depression was taking its toll out in the Kansas City Missouri area. There was still a few months left before the harsh Kansas City winters would come. Rusty's friends had told him about a Blacksmith shop needing a good second hand man to help with shoeing many horses before winter sets in. The job was located in Wichita Kansas and Rusty only had a couple of days to get there or he could be taking a chance of losing out on getting the job he desperately needed to get him through the long winter months. So he set up his wagon and his team of oxen and then started to set out for the two day journey that he had to make.

CHAPTER # 2

RUSTY HAD JUST FINISHED PACKING FOR HIS LONG journey to Wichita Kansas he kissed his bride and set out to be away for at least a few months so he could return home before the long winter months hit. He was leaving in such a hurry Rusty wasn't able to check out the damage to his wagon during the last major storm. Rusty had traveled several hours down the old dirt pathways formed by other pioneers that set off on their own journeys. Rusty came to the end of his first day of traveling he knew it was going to be night fall shortly so he had to find a place to camp and build a fire to cook his dinner. After dinner he had a couple of more chores to do before bedtime. He had to feed the oxen and gather up wood so he could have a fire all night long also he had to set up his bedding close to the fire so he could stay warm. Nights on the open range became rather cool to sleep under the stars. Rusty felt very uneasy about camping out miles away from home with the thought of wild animals lurking in the wilderness. During the night time hours Rusty was awakened by the sounds of howling wolves he knew they were only a feet away from his campsite so that he kept close by to protect himself from these wild creatures. A few minutes later the wolves entered his campsite and ram sacked all of his belongings and managed to take off with all of his food.

The only food Rusty had left was the beef Jerky that his wife had packed in his coat pocket. He figured that he would just have to live on what he had because he didn't have time to go hunting for more food he was still in a hurry to get to Wichita Kansas so he could have a chance to get the job he desperately needed and he only had one more day to get there. Later that day Rusty made it to Wichita He rented a cheap hotel room and went and applied for the job Rusty was granted the job and he devoted most all of his time to his work and Jonathan the Blacksmith owner knew he had made the right choice for the job.

Rusty loved working at the blacksmith shop and he cared deeply about the animals. He was so good to all the animals that he could shoe many horses in just one day. He was making good money working at the shop and it was paying for his room as well as saving some back to survive through the winter. Soon the months were going by and Rusty knew he had to be getting ready to go back to the farm so he could be with his beloved bride Shari and also to get the farmstead ready for the long winter months.

CHAPTER # 3

Back on the farmstead Shari was taking care of things while her husband was out of town. She knew she had lots of chores to do everyday and as soon as her chores were finished she would invite a few of her friends over for some coffee cake that she had just finished baking. Her friends were named Katie, Judy, Mary, and Laura. Sometimes Mary couldn't make it over to her house on account of she was a mid wife and had to take care of all the women in the town and on rare occasions even the men since she was the only one that had experience in the medical field. Katie, Judy and Laura came over to visit and they had such a good time that the day was getting late and Katie, Judy, and Laura knew they had to be getting back their own homes so they could get started on cooking dinner for their own husbands. While Shari was at home cooking dinner she got nauseated and had a sudden dizzy feeling and started to pass out. When her friend Judy came back she found her friend Shari passed out on the floor. Judy hurried to find her friend Mary to come over to Shari's house to find out what was wrong with her.

Mary examined Shari and found out she was pregnant. Shari was so excited about the news that she could hardly wait for her husband to return home so she could tell him the good news. Her friends were also excited about the news of Shari's pregnancy that they would come over to her house everyday to help her out with the chores. Soon the days and months went by and it was mid November Shari went into labor and her friend Mary came over to be with her so she wouldn't be home by herself until the baby was born. Shari felt bad because she was going to have this baby without the presence of her husband. As the day went on the contractions were coming closer. Mary got a hold of Katie, Judy and Laura to inform them that their friend Shari was about ready to give birth to her child so they could be there for the occasion. It was late afternoon and Shari gave birth to a 7 lb. 5 oz baby girl she was just the sweetest thing they had ever saw and that she named this sweet little girl Candy. Katie, Judy, Laura and Mary were so proud of Shari and her baby Candy that they just wanted to hold the baby all the rest of the day. Soon Katie, Laura and Judy went home so they could get their own chores done and dinner before their own husbands returned home from their long day at work.

Mary didn't have a husband so she stayed with Shari to help her out with the chores and the new baby until Shari was rested up and could handle things on her own. Shari knew if she needed help from her friends they would be there for her and to help out anyway they could. Weeks went by and Shari knew her husband would be getting ready for his trip back home to the farm. Shari and her friend Mary wanted to fix up the house with new curtains and to rearrange the furniture. Shari just wanted everything to be perfect when her husband arrived home after months of being gone. Shari's friends also wanted everything to be perfect for her when her husband returned home. Katie, Judy, and Laura also wanted put their own perfection to help out with the home coming. Katie being a basket maker made all sorts of baskets for her friend to decorate her house. Judy for being a dress maker made her friend Shari the most beautiful dress you could ever imagine. Laura being a baker baked all kinds of breads and a special cake for the occasion.

Chapter # 4

IT WAS LATE NOVEMBER AND RUSTY STARTED PACKING ALL his belongings including his food and placed them in his wagon and hitched up his team of oxen for his long journey home. Rusty soon set off on the old dirt pathway for the two day journey back home. Soon Rusty came to the end of the first day of traveling and he found a nice camping spot and shortly fell asleep around the campfire. Morning came and Rusty was becoming very anxious about getting home so he loaded up the wagon and hurried down the old dirt trail. It was late afternoon and Rusty made it to this area that had lots of hills to cross. Rusty still hadn't checked out his wagon for damage from the storm. He went about halfway through this area of big hills when the front wheel of his wagon started to wobble. Rusty was still very excited about getting home he just ignored the wobbling and continued on his way he went about two miles and came to this area that had very rough terrain and very deep ravines. Rusty still continued down the dirt trail when he came upon the edge of one of these deep ravines he tried hard to stop the wagon in such a hurry that the front wheel broke off and the wagon began to slide off into the ravine. As the wagon tumbled down the ravine the oxen broke loose and Rusty was thrown a few feet down to the bottom of the ravine were he hit his head on a rock and became unconscious.

After a few hours Rusty woke up and discovered his wagon was totally destroyed and his oxen's were gone. Rusty knew if he was going to get home he would have to load only what he could carry and started on his way. Soon a few weeks went by and winter was just starting to set in. The cold north winds started to blow and the first snow of the winter began to fall. A few hours later the winds began to blow harder and the snow was falling at a faster pace and Rusty knew he was walking in a blizzard strength storm. Rusty knew he had to find shelter or he could freeze to death. He had walked less than a mile when he stumbled upon an old deserted cabin the door was unlocked so he entered inside and found some wood and started a fire so he could get warmed up. The cabin wasn't much but it was shelter from the storm. He knew he would have to stay there until the storm let up and the trails were passable again so he could get home to his loving bride. Back on the farmstead his beloved wife Shari was very worried about her husband knowing he should have been home weeks ago. Her friends Mary, Judy, Katie and Laura were also worried about Shari's husband and why he hadn't returned home yet.

Shari was just starting to become very depressed over the disappearance of her husband and her friends knew she was getting herself down so Mary, Judy, Katie, and Laura knew they had to convince their friend that everything would be all right and that her husband knew how to take care of himself during this situation. Shari knew her friends were right and put her hopes and prayers in the hands of God to bring her husband home safely. Another few weeks went by and it was getting closer to Christmas. Shari had her friend Mary comes over to stay with the baby so she could cut down a Christmas tree for her home. Mary contacted Judy, Katie, and Laura to come over to Shari's house to help decorate her home as she still held on to the faith that her husband would be home before Christmas and she wanted every thing to be very nice for her husbands home coming.

There were only two days left before Christmas Eve when Shari started to give up hope of her husband being home for Christmas her friends were also starting to give up hope of his reunion. Mary didn't want to see her friend Shari be at home for Christmas all by herself so she invited her and the baby and her other close friends with their husbands to have Christmas at her house. It was Christmas Eve and Shari was getting Candy and herself ready to go to Mary's house when all of a sudden she heard a noise outside and the front door opened and in came Rusty as he was finally home to be reunited with his beloved wife Shari and their new baby daughter Candy for the best Christmas ever.

SECTION # 2

SECTION 2

CHAPTER # 5

I T WAS THREE YEARS LATER AND RUSTY'S ORDEAL WITH his past was finally over and everything was going rather well for him and his family. It was spring time and the year was March 21, 1815 Rusty knew it was time to get the fields ready for plowing and planting his new crops. For the last three years Rusty's crops were making him good money to provide for his family and he felt that he would have another good year for his crop this year. Spring time also was a good time for his livestock his horse gave birth to a new fowl and his cow also gave birth and even his wife Shari was about ready to give birth to their second child. Rusty felt so blessed that God was making his life so fulfilled.

The month was April and Shari gave birth to their new daughter which they named her ruth and again her best friends Mary, Judy, Katie, and Laura were with her during the occasion of the birth of their new baby and best of all her husband was also present. Judy, Katie, and Laura went home and told their husbands that their was going to be a celebration at Rusty's and Shari's farm to celebrate the new blessings of the new season.

Mary and Judy helped decorate the barn while Shari and Katie cooked all kinds of food and Laura baked her special breads and pies for the gathering and they all celebrated until the late night hours.

Morning came and Rusty began to plow and plant up the fields Rusty even had a couple more acres of land to produce his crops. It came towards the end of the spring time and the rains became less frequent as to a start of a drought. Rusty and all the other farmers were worried about their crops for the fear of no rain. Rusty was blessed to live near a creek in which he dug an irrigation route to water his fields during the dry spell. Soon weeks went by and still no rain and Rusty was worried about the creek drying up and that most of the other farmers had already lost all their produce to the lack of rain. Rusty knew that the loss of all his crops would put a huge strain on the economy.

Kansas City was having its worst drought in more than fifty years. The drought was putting a very hard strain on all the people of the town and soon business were starting to fold up and the Kansas city area was taking its toll on the people as they were starting to head off to different areas in order to find a more suitable place to settle but what the people didn't know was that the drought effected over 2/3rds of the country and that left the people less certain where to go to escape the drought. All the people of the town got together for a very important meeting. Everyone decided to stay were they are and to stick it out during the hard times ahead of them. They knew if they would all stick together and believe in their faith that they would survive.

Chapter # 6

S OON THE FALL TIME BEGAN TO SET IN AND THE MONTH
was October and there still wasn't any rain. The farmers
were all worried about the winter months and if there
would still be a drought. During the harsh last six months all the people
of the town was starting to run out of food and supplies that they had
stored up during their good past three years. Soon all the people of
Kansas City started to fear for their town that business's and factories
would began to shut down on account of there would be nothing to sell
or any resources to keep the factories open. The Kansas City area was
going through one of the worst climate changes since the town was
established.

The people of the town feared for the worst as they watched their
town slowly becoming a desolate ghost town. They also feared for some
of the people that they might be packing up all of their own personal
belongings and leaving everything they worked very hard for other
unknown destinations as well as their friends of many years. Even after
all the thoughts of what might happen to the people and their town
even still all the people of the community could still put all their hopes
and prayers in Gods hands and held on to their faith that a miracle just
might come to their town. The people decided that they should stay
and spend as much possible time together as they could and they all
donated some of their own food and supplies together and had a very
big celebration of good friends, and their new destinations.

Soon the winter months came and all the people of the town prepared themselves for whatever kinds of hardships that might be heading their way and to still be able to hold on to the very strong faiths that they had and believed with all their hearts that they would all survive through this ordeal. The month of December had arrived and it was only a few days before Christmas and God answered all the prayers and cries of the people. That night the people of the town heard the thunder and saw the lightning that God had provided an abundant amount of rain and snow storms to fill up all the creeks and rivers and to soften up all the land for next spring's crops. Spring time finally came and the year was March16, 1816 and all of the farmers of the town were very busy plowing and planting up their fields. Soon the crops began to grow and that they were getting plenty of rain for their fields and all the people of the community felt very blessed and happy they made it through another hard turbulence in their lives and the people of the Kansas city learned not to take anything for granted.

CHAPTER # 7

SOON ALL THE PEOPLE OF KANSAS CITY AREA FELT VERY blessed that their town was starting to grow again and that more business's were booming and the economy was starting to improve over just a few months. Soon other settlers heard about how the Kansas City area was growing and wanted to be a part of their town and soon more settlers were beginning to move in by the hundreds and soon more buildings and farmsteads were being established and the Kansas City area became a full size town. Its been two years since the big boom and the growth of the Kansas City area that finally their town grew big enough that they were going to be granted a railroad line going right though the middle of their town.

All the people of the town were very excited about the news that they all decided to have a big celebration for this very special occasion. Also the town recently acquired a port on the river and large boats to haul their goods up and down the river from St. Joseph to St. louis Missouri. Factories also grew along the river and the Kansas City areas economy was at its highest rate ever.

SECTION # 3

CHAPTER # 8

TEN YEARS WENT BY SINCE THE TOWN GREW AND IT was springtime and the year is March 30, 1826. Rusty his wife Shari and the girls Candy and ruth were having a very good year the crops were growing in the fields and the girls were being home schooled by their mother. Shari enjoyed teaching her daughters to read and write and all the other valuable things there were to learn. Shari still kept in touch with her best friends Laura, Katie, Judy, and Mary. Sometimes Mary couldn't always be with her friends.

Mary earned her Doctrine Certificate and opened up her own clinic to practice medicine. She was always very busy with all the people's health Katie's basket making was going so well with her that she opened a little shop to sell her baskets. She was selling up to three baskets a day and making a very good income for herself. Laura's bakery business was also starting to become a very big success for her that she decided to open up a bakery shop of her own so she could sell her goods to the public. Since the Kansas City area was growing and more folks were settling in and that meant more ladies that were in demand for new dresses that Judy had to hire a helper to help with her dress making business. The Kansas City areas economy was now at its highest rate since the year of 1815. The people were very proud to live in their town.

Chapter # 9

———————

T HE KANSAS CITY AREA WAS DOING SO WELL THAT the population began to grow at large numbers and that meant more children that needed to have a place to get an education a luxury that most of the parents had to do without to help provide for their families. The town took a vote and decided to build a building that would be suitable enough to become a school as well as a place of worship. The new building was finally finished and now it was time to find a good teacher to teach the children how to read and write. The people of town knew of only one member in their community who was qualified to provide that kind of education to their kids. Shari gratefully took the job to become the town's teacher

She was so excited to know that she could make such an impact on the community and that she could even have her own schoolhouse. Shari's friends Mary, Laura, Katie and Judy were also very excited for her blessing. When Jonathan the blacksmith shop owner in Wichita Kansas heard about how the Kansas City area was growing that he decided to move his blacksmith and livery shop to Kansas City. He found a very nice piece of land around the river area were his livestock could have plenty of water to drink. Jonathan realized that his business was far to great for him to tend to all the needs of the livestock on his own. He needed to hire a couple of farm hands to help him with the animals.

He asked Rusty to see if he would be interested in working for him at the livery. He knew Rusty had a love for animals and how great he was with them. Rusty was so excited about the job he didn't even hesitate to accept the job that he loved so much. Rusty knew of another man that was desperate about finding a job so he told Jonathan about his friend Pio. Jonathan went and talked to Pio about working at the livery stable to help out with the animals and Pio was excited and accepted the job. Both Rusty and Pio were very experienced to care for the livestock and all of their needs. Now all the people of the town were all blessed to know that their town had everything they needed to be complete.

SECTION # 4

CHAPTER # 10

FIFTEEN YEARS HAS PASSED BY AND THE YEAR WAS August 16, 1841. The Kansas City area was still going strong and the population was in the thousands. Some of the residence of the town was owners of their own business's while others were fortunate to have jobs working for other people but still the majority of the people were active farmers farming their own land and raising their own livestock. Rusty and Shari were also meeting a new milestone in their lives Candy and ruth were grown young ladies starting off with their own lives. The girls were setting off to go to college to follow in their mothers footsteps and also to become teachers.

It was springtime and the year was May 10, 1843 and the ladies Candy and ruth were heading back to the farmstead to put their teaching certificates to work for them. Since there weren't a lot of teachers in their community they started off with their careers immediately after graduation. One hot afternoon in the month of June Candy and ruth were just leaving the schoolhouse for the evening. ruth had asked Candy if she would like to have a ride home in her new horse and buggy from the money that she had saved. Candy had told her sister that she felt like walking home and her sister ruth Knew she just loved the countryside. Candy was walking along the trail when she encountered a new man in town. Candy was so overwhelmed over this man that she continued to walk along the trail in hopes to run across him again. Three days later Candy was walking down the trail and was lucky enough to run across this man again. She slowed down as he calmly approached her and introduced himself to her his name was Kyle. All the rest of the afternoon Kyle and Candy sat under a shade tree and talked and got to know a great deal of each other. When Candy got home she told her mother and sister the good news about the man she met on the trail. Her mother and sister were so happy to see the glow in Candy's face for she was in love with this man Kyle. Time swiftly went by and Kyle and Candy got seeing a lot of each other. Kyle knew in his heart that Candy was the lady of his dreams that he was going to propose his engagement to her and for her to become his bride. Candy was so excited that she didn't even hesitate to say yes. Rusty and Shari and her sister ruth were so happy to hear the news that they all gave their blessings to both Kyle and Candy and granted Kyle with their daughter in marriage and also welcomed Kyle as a new member of the family and they all celebrated the occasion. Soon all the people of the town heard the news of Kyle's and Candy's blessings to be married that the whole town was very happy for the both of them. Shari's best friends Katie, Judy, Laura, and Mary were also very excited for the big news.

CHAPTER # 11

THE TIME CAME FOR EVERYONE TO GET PREPARED FOR Kyle and Candy's wedding. Rusty and Shari was busy getting the barn ready while Katie was busy making all kinds of baskets and Laura was busy baking all kinds of breads and rolls including the wedding cake and Judy was also busy making a very beautiful dress for Candy to wear on her wedding day. Mary helped Shari with the cooking of all the food they needed for the big feast. Everyone was so excited to be helping out with this very special day. Kyle and a few of his friends were also very busy decorating his wagon with all kinds of flowers and strings of cans tied to the back of the wagon as well as a banner that read just married. When they finished the wagon it was the most prettiest wagon you could ever imagine. Finally everything was ready for the ceremony to begin. They had so many family members and friends that the barn was full of people to witness the happiest day of Kyle and Candy's new life as husband and wife. Kyle had told his bride that he had one more surprise for her to see and Kyle's friends Roger and Jeff rode up in his fully decorated wagon for the newlywed couple to ride off for their honeymoon. Everyone gathered around the wagon to throw rice at the couple as they rode away down the trail it was a very nice occasion for all the folks that day. While the newlywed couple was away the people of the town all wanted to show their gratitude to the new couple that everyone chipped in and purchased a few acres of land and built a very nice cabin and barn for Kyle and Candy to call home. When Kyle and Candy returned back to the Rusty's and Shari's farm all the people of the town were so very excited to show the new couple what they all had done for them and Kyle and Candy knew that they were blessed to live in a community that had very caring people in it.

SECTION # 5

CHAPTER # 12

TWO YEARS WENT BY FOR THE NEW COUPLE AND THE year was 1845 and Kyle and Candy was preparing for their first child. Rusty and Shari was also preparing for their next milestone a grandfather and a grandmother they were both very excited about the news. The year was October 23, 1847 and Candy gave birth to a 5lb 12oz baby boy. The new parents named their son Isaiah Once again Shari's friends Mary, Katie, Judy and Laura were at Shari's and Rusty's house for the occasion of their first grandchild. A few years went by and Rusty and Shari once again looked back at years since they first married and knew they were blessed again. It was summertime and the year was June 4, 1852. Things were starting to change again for Rusty and Shari that their daughters were grown and were about ready for their own lives and journeys. A few of their friends were about to start their own new destinations. Their youngest daughter ruth was offered a teaching job in Springfield Missouri and that she just couldn't pass up the opportunity and also Mary was offered a job in New York City to become a Chief of staff in a teaching Hospital. Katie and her husband set off west on the hopes of becoming rich from the California gold rush they had spent six months hoping for their dreams to happen and then they came back to the Kansas City area. Judy also had big demands for the making of her dresses that everything become a huge success for her that she opened up her own seamstress company and hired a crew to help out with all of her orders. Laura was happy about staying in the Kansas City area that she opened up her own bakery warehouse and she hired a crew to help her out with all of her bakery orders that she shipped out nationwide. Soon the time came for Kyle,

Candy and their son Isaiah to start packing up all their belongings and also to get prepared for their long journey to the west in search for their new destination as well as their new way of life. Everyone felt so blessed with their lives they knew they had the best of everything that a town could provide and many years of good friends and pleasures.

SECTION # 6

(PART TWO)
THE NEXT GENERATION

CHAPTER # 13

I T WAS EARLY SPRING AND THE YEAR WAS MAY 26, 1860.
Kyle had received an urgent telegram from the railroad
company offering him a job in Portland Oregon. He knew
he should take the job because it was going to pay him good money
to provide for his family. When he arrived home he was so excited to
tell his wife about the good news of his new job offer. He explained to
his wife that the job was in Oregon and that they would have to start
packing up all their belongings and get ready for their long journey they
had to make. While Kyle was getting the wagon and his team of horses
ready for the trip Candy and Isaiah went to her Dad and mom's home
to tell them about the news of Kyle's new job. She also told them that
the job was in Oregon and that they would have to be getting things
ready to relocate. Rusty and Shari were very excited for the good news
about the job but were sad that their daughter and son in law would
be leaving to a very far place to call home. Rusty and Shari knew how
important the job was and accepted the news as well as any parent could.
Kyle, Candy, and Isaiah spent as much time as they could with her folks
until the time came for their departure. Kyle's friends Roger, Jeff, and
Pio were also excited about the new job that they chipped in and helped
Kyle get ready for their long journey.

Kyle figured that the trip would probably would take four or five
months to get their . They both discussed the trip to each other and
tried to prepare themselves for all things that they might experience on
the way. Soon the big day came for the young pioneers Rusty and Shari
decided to have a big celebration and invited a few of their friends to
celebrate the occasion. After the celebration was over everyone chipped

in to help Kyle load up his wagon with all the necessary items they might need until they reached their destination. Kyle, Candy, and Isaiah said all their goodbyes to all their family and friends and set down the old paths for a new life in a new place.

SECTION # 7

CHAPTER # 14

D AYS WENT BY SINCE KYLE, CANDY AND ISAIAH LEFT the Kansas City Missouri area after traveling all day they came to this very beautiful valley somewhere in Kansas and decided to set up camp. While Candy was already preparing to fix dinner for her family Kyle was unleashing the horses from the wagon to take them out to the nice valley to graze on the tall green grass. Isaiah went off to do his own sightseeing and had wondered away from the camp. Soon Isaiah realized he was lost and was just walking around in circles trying to find the campsite. Isaiah was lost in the big valley. He knew it would be dark soon and he had to find shelter before nightfall. Isaiah learned a lot from his father about being separated from the family during their long journey.

Kyle soon came back to the campsite after tending to the horses. Candy had mentioned to her husband that Isaiah hasn't returned from his hike and that it would be dark soon and he should have been back at the camp by now. Candy was very worried about their son being lost in the middle of nowhere and that Kyle was getting ready to go out and search for their son. Candy knew that Kyle always gave their son advice in what to do in case of an emergency. Isaiah soon found an old cave that he could stay the night in and gathered up as much wood as he could find to make a fire for him to stay warm during the long night hours.

Soon morning came and Isaiah knew he had to find his way back to his family. He went about 100 feet from the cave entrance and noticed a patch of blackberries and he was very hungry that he just walked right over to those berries and started to help himself when all of a sudden he heard this grunting sound he looked up and there stood a six foot

300 lbs black bear right in front of him. Isaiah got scared and he took off running to get away from the bear. When Isaiah looked back the bear was only a few feet behind him. Isaiah started to run faster when he tripped and fell over a log that was in his path. Seconds later Isaiah was being pounced on and battered by this very angry bear. Isaiah yelled and fought to get the bear off him Kyle had already set off in search for their lost son. He had only gone about two miles west of the campsite when he heard yelling and growling sounds and when he turned around he saw that this bear was all over their son he quickly took out his rifle and shot and killed the bear before it killed their son. Kyle ran over to their son and found Isaiah had only suffered few scratches and bruises and a few minor cuts Kyle knew their son was a very lucky boy. Kyle went over to his wagon and got out the rope he always carried with him they tied up the bear and took it back to the camp with them and they knew it could have a very good use to them while on their trip.

SECTION # 8

Chapter # 15

WEEKS WENT BY SINCE THE YOUNG PIONEER FAMILY set out on their way they were somewhere in South Dakota when they came to this place of very rugged and rough ravines and rugged steep formations and deep craters that it made passing through this area would be a challenge to cross and it caused them to venture a few days off their route to get around this very difficult region. Several more weeks went by for this family and it was the peak of the rainy season. The rain fell for days and the trails were getting very muddy that made traveling harder for the team of horses to climb the hills. Kyle decided to stay on the trail in the valley area to make up lost time.

Soon Kyle, Candy, and Isaiah came up to this big river. Kyle knew he would have to find a place were they could cross safely in order to get to the other side and with all the rain they had the river was up. As they rode along the river they came to this area that looked a little more promising to try and cross the rain had finally stopped and they decided to set up camp so the horses could rest and graze on the green grass. While Kyle and Isaiah were busy finishing up with nightly chores Candy was preparing to fix dinner for her hungry family as they had planned to cross the river the next day. Kyle and Candy knew that they could experience a very rough ordeal and to prepare them for whatever might be thrown at them. Kyle, Candy and Isaiah believed that everything would be fine. Kyle and his family had very strong faith that God would get them through this. Soon morning came while Kyle and Isaiah was busy hitching up the team and securing their personal belongings to the wagon Candy was busy preparing food for their trip and cleaning up the campsite. She was always so observant to make sure every emit of the campfire was out before leaving on their courageous adventure to Oregon.

CHAPTER # 16

W<small>HILE EVERYTHING WAS SECURED AND EVERYONE</small> was braced Kyle gave the team the OK to move out first one axle then the other. Soon the wagon and the team was moving smoothly towards the other side Kyle and Candy became a little more relaxed. They got about a third of the way across the river when they noticed the water was beginning to rise along the sides of the wagon and the current was stronger the further they went. Kyle knew that he would have to really fight the team to keep them going straight.

Once again the wagon and the team were going fairly smooth. While Isaiah was observing the water around the sides of the wagon he looked to the right and noticed a big log floating towards them in the rivers current. Kyle swiftly tried to slow the team but the log managed to float behind the team and got hung up under the wagon. Kyle knew that he had to do something to free the log from the front wheel. He had to climb into the swift current of the river and was trying to push the log away from the wheel with one hand while the other hand was holding on to the wagon so he wouldn't float away in the current.

After two or three hard pulls Kyle managed to free the log and as it was floating down the river in the current Kyle noticed the wagon was beginning to float in the current as he tried to climb up the wheel so he could take control of the team that his foot had slipped and caused him to fall into the swift current and managed to grab hold of the wheel as he tried to pull himself from the river. Isaiah realized that his father was having a hard time pulling himself from the strong current so he hurried over to the side of the wagon and grabbed a hold of his father's jacket and pulled his father right out of the river. Kyle was very proud of Isaiah that his father considered him a man for his fast thinking to save him. Isaiah was proud of his father for considering him as a man. Isaiah loved his father that he would do just about anything to help out his family. Everything started to go alright for Kyle and his family as they came to the other side of the river and was safely on dry ground again. Night fall was coming shortly so this pioneer family found a place to set up camp as they were all tired and that the team needed to graze and rest after all their hard work they managed to do. After all the chores were done the family praised God for their courage and faith they had to get across the river safely.

SECTION # 9

CHAPTER # 17

A FEW MONTHS WENT BY WHEN KYLE, CANDY, AND Isaiah finally made the end of their journey as they arrived in Portland Oregon in late October 1860. Kyle knew winter would be coming soon and that they would have to be purchasing some land to build a cabin to wait out the long winter months. Kyle and Isaiah knew they would have to work hard and fast if they were going to get the cabin liveable before the hard snowfalls would come. Everyone knew that the Oregon winters were cold and harsh. Soon the cabin was finished and they had a large pile of wood to burn in the fireplace to keep them warm. It was November 5 1860 and this pioneer family had just settled for the long winter months. Soon the snow started and it snowed clear up to the springtime. It was mid June 1861 the winter had finally became springtime and Kyle was getting ready for his first day of work on the railroad. He soon met up with a bunch of guys that was going to be the part of the blasting team. These guys were Kyle, Smitty, Ely, Angel, romy and Mike. They all had to trust each other if they were going to make this very dangerous job work for their safety. Their responsibility was to blast out portions of the cave for the tracks to be laid by the other group of guys the track layers. Weeks went by and the foreman was being pressured by the railroad company to get more feet of blasting done a day. The foreman came to Kyle and told him that he had to get his crew to blast more feet per day. Kyle talked to his team and told them they would have to use more dynamite in holes they chiseled out. Soon everything was going fine they were blasting out an additional five feet of rock a day. It was a new day for the blasting team and Ely one of the crew members decided that he wanted to speed up the job so he chiseled his hole a little deeper so he could load more dynamite to produce a bigger blast. Kyle found out what Ely was up to and warned him of the dangers he could inflict on all the other crew members lives. Ely just wouldn't listen and took matters in his own hands Ely started shoving the dynamite into the hole and without any warning Ely set off the charge and it was the biggest blast that it literally shook the walls of the cave and started to crumble trapping all the blasting team in the cave including himself.

The crew was very furious about what Ely had done and started a big up roar with him as they all feared for their lives. Kyle knew that the energy the crew was using on Ely could be used for trying to dig their selves out. Kyle also knew that every one would have to work as a team if they were going to get out alive. Hours went by and everyone was exhausted from digging rock and dirt from the cave. The oxygen was also getting harder to breath for the team. Kyle knew he had to continually encourage the team to keep up their faith that every thing was going to be all right and the team kept on digging. Soon a few more hours went by and some of the crew member were getting very disoriented from the lack of oxygen that some were on the verge of passing out. Kyle was a very big believer of his faith that he gathered up the crew from their work to pray for all their safety and that a miracle would save their lives. Thirty minutes later the crew heard a sound of shovels just outside the wall of rocks and dirt that they started to dig in a way that they haven't ever dug before with joy and excitement. Soon the diggers from both sides of the wall started to form a big hole as they met in the middle and soon all the crew members were rescued and outside of the cave and were safe and no lives were lost that day.

It was late September and the year was 1862 two years later from the blasting of the cave. The job was finally finished and the tracks were laid and ready for use. Kyle knew his work was completed so he and his family went back to the cabin they build and decided to do some farming and to teach their son how to farm as well. Kyle knew that he had a lot of work to do around the farm to get prepared for another long harsh snowy winter.

SECTION # 10

CHAPTER # 18

———◦((◦))◦———

SOON SPRINGTIME CAME AND IT WAS LATE MAY AND THE year was 1863. Kyle knew it was time to teach Isaiah to become a man and learn the farming business. Isaiah had a very deep love for animals that he took after the footsteps of his grandfather who also had a deep love for animals. Isaiah always helped his father around the farm. He went to the barn to hitch the horses to the plowing equipment. Isaiah was ready to learn from his father to plow up the land for planting. Soon the land was ready to begin planting the crops. Kyle was very proud of his son Isaiah that he knew he had the best farm helper anyone could ever ask for. Isaiah knew he had a very busy day and after cleaning himself up and had ate his dinner he was ready for bed to get ready for another hard day of learning to farm the land. Morning came and after a good breakfast Kyle and Isaiah were heading out to the fields for a long day of planting the crops.

They were going to plant half of the field with corn and the other half with wheat since they were the highest demand for the crop industries. Isaiah was very happy to know that he had accomplished the knowledge of farming and knowing that he had a lot to do with the fields and the crops this season. Isaiah was so proud of the crops he spent a lot of time taking care of the fields. He made sure the irrigation channels were always free of anything that could stop the water flow from watering the fields. It was late September 1863 Kyle and Isaiah were excited about their day on account it was harvest day. They both knew they had a very nice yield this season and that would make them enough money to get through the winter months. After Kyle and Isaiah started to harvest the crops Kyle noticed some smoke in the far distance but he just ignored it and helped his son harvest the crops.

Several hours went by and Kyle noticed the smoke was getting closer so Kyle and Isaiah worked as fast as they could to harvest all the crops. Soon the smoke was at the far end of their field Kyle knew their was a wild fire heading their way so he mentioned to Isaiah to unhitch the horses from the plow and to head up to the cabin so they could start to gather up everything they could load on their wagon to survive on. While Isaiah and Candy were loading the wagon Kyle was inspecting the team of horses to see if they were in good shape for traveling they had to evacuate the cabin as soon as possible. Finally they were heading down the trail as they looked back to see that the wildfire had started on their farm and consumed their crops and watched their cabin burn up as well. Soon this pioneer family felt as though they had lost a lot but realized they still had each other and that they were blessed that day. Kyle talked it over with Candy and Isaiah and decided to go back to Kansas City Missouri so they were preparing for their long journey back home to surprise their family of their return.

SECTION # 11

(PART # 3)
THE RETURN

CHAPTER # 19

I T WAS LATE FALL AND WHILE KYLE AND ISAIAH WERE busy loading their wagon with the things they were able to sacrifice from the fire Candy was cooking food for their trip over a campfire. Soon the chores were finished and the pioneer family was ready to travel their long journey home to Kansas City. Kyle knew it would be winter soon and that they would have to stop and build a cabin and to cut some wood and also hunt for a large moose for food so they could stick out the weather till spring. It was May 1864 spring has finally arrived and it was time for Kyle to take his family on the rest of the long journey. While Kyle and his family were somewhere in the state of Utah Isaiah noticed a pack of wolves lurking in the distance. Suddenly the wolves started to move out of the tree line and in to the open area. Kyle knew he had to act fast to keep the hungry wolves from getting the horses. The pack of wolves started running towards the pioneer family so Kyle started to run the horses as fast as they would go but the hungry wolves were keeping up and starting to surround their wagon. Kyle told Isaiah to get the rest of the meat from the storage box and throw it out to the wolves so that it could buy them some time for their safe get away. This pioneer family was finally on their way to finish their long journey back.

It was early August and Kyle and his family was safely back in Kansas City Missouri. Kyle knew he wanted to purchase some land to build a cabin before notifying the rest of the family members of their return. It was early September Kyle and Isaiah had finished building the cabin and the barn for the horses and also gathered a large wood pile that would get them through the winter. Kyle and Isaiah also knew they would have to go hunting to provide the family with meat for most of the winter months. Kyle and Isaiah had came across this very huge mule deer staring right at them Kyle always knew he wanted to teach his son to hunt so he handed the riffle to Isaiah and told him to shoot the deer Isaiah was very uneasy about shooting the deer at first but his father told him he was very confident that he would do fine so Isaiah shot and killed the deer right where it stood. Isaiah knew that his father had made a man of him and that he was proud of his father and that his father was very blessed to have a son like Isaiah. It was spring time the year was June 1865 Kyle and his family went to make it known to his family that they were back for good. Rusty and Shari were so happy to get the good news of their return that she notified all of her friends she told Laura, Judy, and Katie the good news of her families return she just couldn't tell her friend Mary because she was so far away and had been gone for years in New York City, New York.

SECTION # 12

CHAPTER # 20

——➤◀«(❂)»▶——

SHARI, JUDY, LAURA , AND KATIE DECIDED THAT THEY should have a celebration to welcome Kyle and his family back. While Shari and Judy went to let the people of the town know that they were planning a big festival to be in their town. Laura she went back to her bakery shop and started to make the rolls, pies and cakes and anything else she could think of because Laura loved to bake for any reason there was to do so. Katie she loved her basket making business that she also went and got busy making baskets of all sizes and shapes. Judy she had the love of making beautiful dresses that she went back to her dress shop and made many dresses of all styles.

Shari loved everything about festivals and celebrations that she enjoyed making the decorations. While she was preparing the decorations she was thinking about how much she missed her friend Mary because she always helped Shari with making pretty decorations and all of the different kinds of flower arrangements. All the people of the town were also busy helping to get the festival ready for the big day. The ladies were busy making gifts of all sorts. Some were making crafts while others were making all kinds of different candies and all kinds of different jams. The men of the town were very busy with the building huts and planning setups for the festivities. Mary heard about the festival for the return of Kyle, Candy, and Isaiah homecoming she also heard that the growth rate of people in the Kansas City was way over the Thousands and needed a new Doctor to join the firm. Mary excitingly accepted the position and thought she would surprise all her best friends of her return back To Kansas city.

As soon as Mary got off the train she entered the depot and boarded the stagecoach which took her to the area were all her friends are. Mary hurried over to Shari 's Place and Shari was so excited to see her friend that the tears were falling down her face. Shari notified Judy, Laura, and Katie of Mary's homecoming they all rushed over to visit with Mary. Shari and Rusty got a telegram stating that ruth their other daughter was coming back to Kansas City for a new teaching job. Shari and Rusty were so blessed to have all their family members back home again they all celebrated till the late night hours. The day arrived of the festival for the town and everyone showed up and they all had the best time anyone could have to be proud that they all lived in Kansas City and every year they always had big festival for all occasions. They all agreed that Kansas City was the best place to live.